T-REX

BACK TO THE CRETACEOUS

Imax Presents

T-REX
BACK TO THE CRETACEOUS

By Ruth Ashby

From a Screenplay by
Andrew Gellis and Jeanne Rosenberg
Story by Andrew Gellis and David Young

A Byron Preiss Visual
Publications, Inc. Book

■SCHOLASTIC

New York   Toronto   London   Auckland   Sydney
Mexico City   New Delhi   Hong Kong

Designed by Dean Motter

Library of Congress Cataloging-in-Publication Data
Ashby, Ruth
Imax Presents T-REX: BACK TO THE CRETACEOUS / by Ruth Ashby
        p. cm.
    "A Byron Preiss book."
    ISBN 0-439-15341-7
    1. Dinosaurs—Juvenile literature. [1. Dinosaurs.] 1. .Ashby, Ruth, ill. II. Title.®

        567.9'1—dc   94-15522
10 9 8 7 6 5 4 3 2 1   0/0 01 02 03 04

Printed in Mexico 49

First printing, August 2000

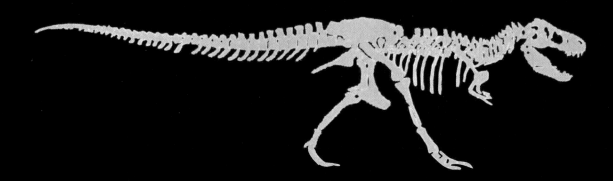

"Hey, Dad, wait up for me!" sixteen-year-old Ally Hayden called out. She hurried down the hall of the dinosaur museum after her father.

Dr. Hayden turned around and grinned. "Don't worry, Ally," he said. "Those dinosaur bones aren't going to walk away."

Dr. Donald Hayden was a paleontologist at the Royal Tyrrell Museum in Alberta, Canada. He had just returned from his yearly dinosaur dig. And Ally couldn't wait to see what he had discovered!

Ally loved dinosaurs more than anything in the whole world. Every summer she worked as a guide at the museum. She had even finished a science project on her favorite dinosaur of all—the awesome *Tyrannosaurus rex*!

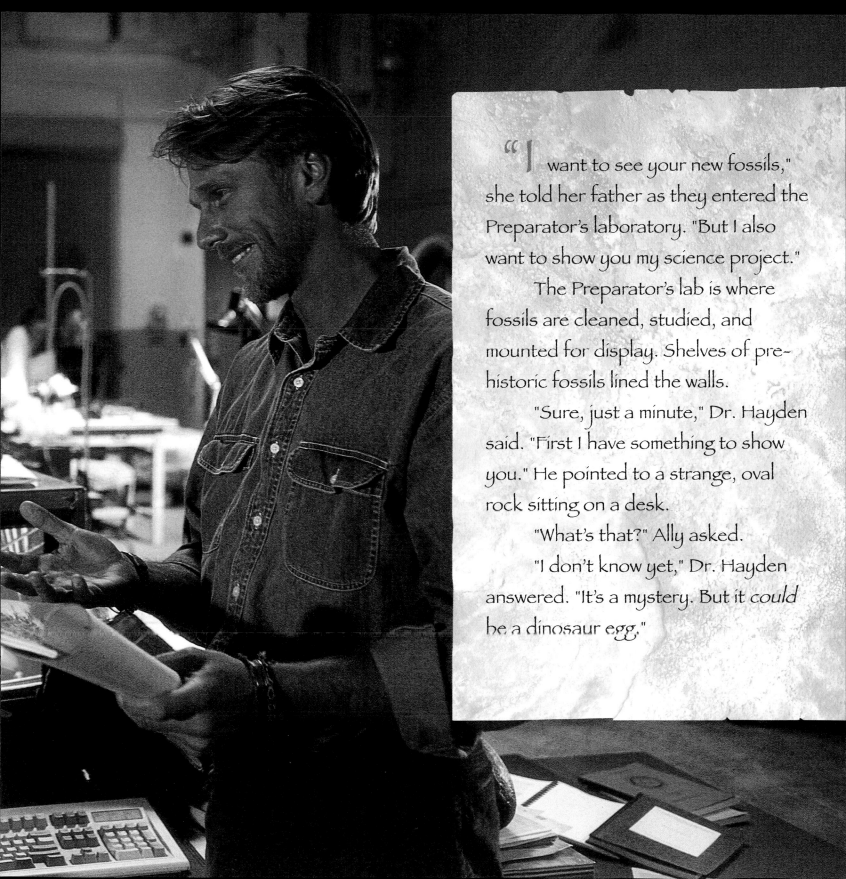

"I want to see your new fossils," she told her father as they entered the Preparator's laboratory. "But I also want to show you my science project."

The Preparator's lab is where fossils are cleaned, studied, and mounted for display. Shelves of pre-historic fossils lined the walls.

"Sure, just a minute," Dr. Hayden said. "First I have something to show you." He pointed to a strange, oval rock sitting on a desk.

"What's that?" Ally asked.

"I don't know yet," Dr. Hayden answered. "It's a mystery. But it *could* be a dinosaur egg."

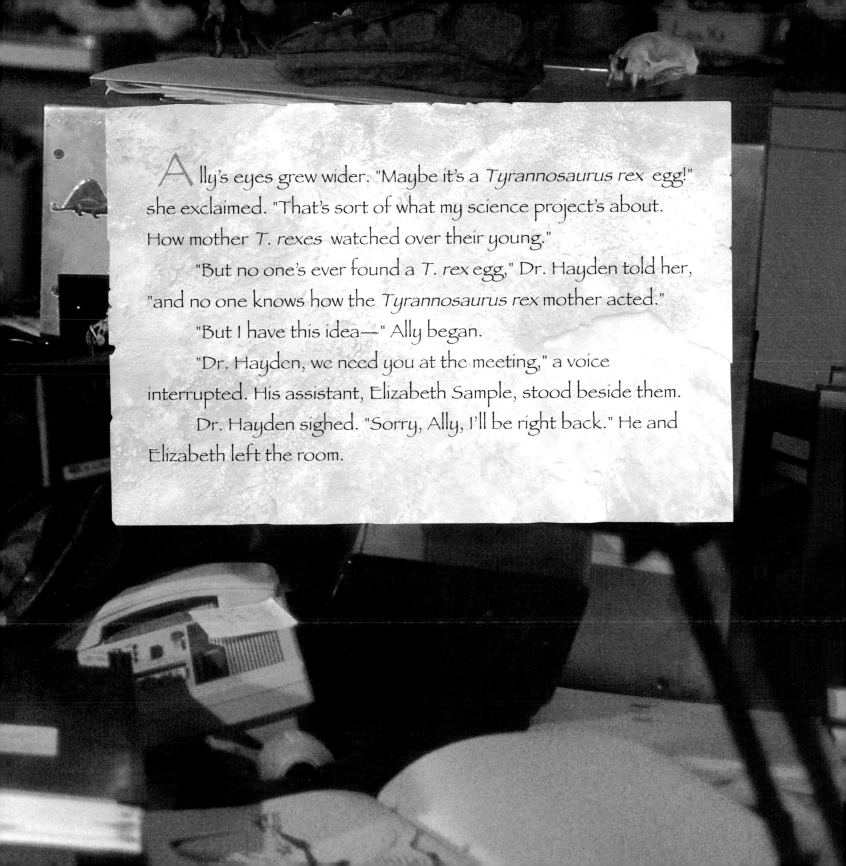

Ally's eyes grew wider. "Maybe it's a *Tyrannosaurus rex* egg!" she exclaimed. "That's sort of what my science project's about. How mother *T. rexes* watched over their young."

"But no one's ever found a *T. rex* egg," Dr. Hayden told her, "and no one knows how the *Tyrannosaurus rex* mother acted."

"But I have this idea—" Ally began.

"Dr. Hayden, we need you at the meeting," a voice interrupted. His assistant, Elizabeth Sample, stood beside them.

Dr. Hayden sighed. "Sorry, Ally, I'll be right back." He and Elizabeth left the room.

Ally was left alone in the Preparator's lab. Suddenly the lights dimmed.

"The museum is now closed," a voice announced over the loudspeaker. "All visitors please leave by the front entrance."

Ally sighed and gazed at the oddly-shaped rock. "I hope it *is* a fossilized egg," she said to herself. "Then maybe we can find out if my idea about *Tyrannosaurus rex* mothers is right."

She reached over to switch on a desk lamp. As she turned, her arm knocked into the fossil.

"Oh, no!" Ally cried.

She watched in horror as the rock teetered on the edge of the desk—and toppled toward the floor!

Crash!

The rock that might once have been a dinosaur egg hit the floor with a loud thump. Ally bent over it to see if there was any damage.

She gasped as a cloud of orange smoke rose from the rock. "Eww!" she cried, covering her nose and mouth with her hand.

The smell was awful. But just as quickly as the smoke came, it disappeared.

Ally felt dizzy. I'd better get some fresh air, she thought. She put the rock back on the desk and stumbled out of the Preparator's lab.

The exhibition hall was dark and full of shadows. All the visitors had left the museum.

"Could I be the only one here?" Ally wondered out loud. Suddenly she heard a sound like a dull roar. It grew louder as she entered the dinosaur halls.

Ally shook her head, trying to clear it. I must be imagining things, she thought. That sounds like the roar of a huge beast!

The roar grew louder and louder. She turned a corner and entered the dinosaur hall. The gigantic skeletons cast eerie shadows on the walls.

Tyrannosaurus rex towered above the rest.

I won't be frightened, Ally decided. She folded her arms and stared straight at the skeleton.

Then something amazing happened. The *T. rex* head turned and looked at her!

Ally was too surprised to move. I didn't really see that, she reassured herself. But as she watched, the skeleton grew muscle. Then skin. Then teeth.

Ally remained frozen in place. And then—

The tyrannosaur lunged right at her!

Ally tried to scream, but she couldn't make a sound. The tyrannosaur's head loomed closer. Its jaws opened wide. She could see its long, pink tongue. She could almost smell its hot breath.

I've got to get out of here! she told herself. Ally took a step back. And another.

Then she turned—and ran.

UPPER HA

As Ally raced down the hall, the museum walls seemed to disappear. It seemed as if she was running through a cloud of color and fog. Objects and scenes began whizzing by her head.

The Leaning Tower of Pisa. The head of Buddha. A statue of an Egyptian pharaoh. Prehistoric cave paintings.

It feels like I'm in some sort of tunnel to the past, Ally thought, like I'm traveling back in time!

Suddenly the moving images stopped. Where am I? she wondered.

Ally looked around. She was standing in the middle of a lush, green jungle. A real jungle—not a museum exhibit.

Wait a minute! She had seen these plants before—in the paintings of Charles Knight, the most famous dinosaur painter who ever lived.

"I can't believe this. I must have traveled back to the Cretaceous," she whispered, "back to the time of *Tyrannosaurus rex*."

This is incredible! Ally thought. Now I know what the Earth looked like sixty-five million years ago!

She began to explore the tropical forest. Lush palm trees and bright tropical flowers surrounded her. She recognized the cycads, primitive trees with thick trunks and fernlike leaves. Long moss-covered vines hung everywhere.

It sure is hot and humid here, Ally said to herself. She brushed a flying insect away from her face. Too bad I didn't bring bug spray!

A bellow rang through the forest. Ally shivered. Her fear was mixed with excitement. Maybe that sound came from a dinosaur. Whatever it was, it was definitely close by.

Ally stepped out from behind a huge fern and stared straight ahead. A herd of hadrosaurs, the duckbilled dinosaurs, was gathered by a lake.

One looked up, right into her eyes.

Ally tried not to feel nervous. Hadrosaurs were plant-eaters, after all. They wouldn't attack her—would they?

Another hadrosaur stopped drinking and gazed at her. Then another. And another.

Ally tried to hide behind a cycad. This can't be happening, she thought. She closed her eyes and tried to force herself back to the present time.

One hadrosaur gave a loud honk. Birds twittered in the trees.

Then all was silent.

Ally opened her eyes. Yes, it worked! She was back in the museum—right in the middle of a jungle exhibit!

And the hadrosaurs had turned back into skeletons again.

"This is all so weird," Ally said out loud. "I've got to find my dad and tell him what's happening." She climbed out of the jungle exhibit and began to search for him.

"Dad!" Ally called out. The sound echoed through the empty halls.

"Ally!" a faint voice replied.

I think the sound is coming from over there, Ally thought, heading over to the Charles Knight exhibit.

She stopped in front of one of Knight's paintings. He was her favorite artist. He had started working at the beginning of the twentieth century. That's when dinosaur hunters like Barnum Brown were carting trainloads of dinosaur bones from dig sites back to museums. Knight had turned the dry bones into living, breathing dinosaurs again—just by painting them!

The two dryptosaurs in the painting were fighting. As Ally watched, they suddenly jumped off the canvas. . .

And kept fighting in midair!

Zap! Suddenly the dryptosaur dinosaurs were behind her. And Ally was in the forest world of the painting.

Here I go again! she thought. She looked around and noticed a serious-looking young man standing at an easel. She walked up behind him and looked at his painting.

"Wow!" she exclaimed. "You're Charles Knight!"

"Do I know you?" Knight asked.

"No, but I really admire your work." Ally leaned closer to the canvas. "You're not always accurate, though. The *T. rex* has two fingers, not three."

"The skeletons Barnum Brown brought back from Red Deer River weren't complete," Knight explained, "so I took a guess."

"Your paintings seem so real," Ally exclaimed. "It's as if you actually knew what dinosaurs looked like."

"Well, I've examined lots of dinosaur skeletons," Knight said, "and I've watched how lots of animals move. With a little imagination, anyone can put himself or herself back in time. You seem to have that ability, too."

As Ally watched, Charles Knight began to shimmer and dissolve . . . .

"Do you really think so, Mr. Knight?" Ally asked. "Mr. Knight?"

But Charles Knight was no longer there, and Ally found herself back in the museum again.

Maybe I'm dreaming, Ally thought, shaking her head. She walked over to the restroom and slowly opened the door. Everything seemed normal. Relieved, she went in and splashed some water on her face. Then she looked up—and found herself outside a tent on a long flatboat. There was a young man staring at a fossilized bone. He was wearing old-fashioned clothing.

The young man looked around. "Can I help you? You look lost."

"I am, kind of," Ally said. "Where are we?"

"Red Deer River, Alberta, Canada, 1910," he replied.

"Then you must be Barnum Brown," Ally said.

"That's the name, bones are the game," Brown replied. "How did you know?"

"Are you kidding?" Ally exclaimed. "You're the most famous bone-digger in history."

Barnum Brown smiled. "The most famous, huh?" he said softly. "Come on, I want to show you something."

Ally followed Brown to the other side of the flatboat. Piles of plaster-wrapped bones were stacked on the deck.

The cliffs of the Red Deer River badlands rose spectacularly on either side.

Wow! I'm on my first field survey! Ally thought excitedly. I bet Barnum Brown can answer some of my questions about *T. rex*.

Brown pointed toward the cliffs. "Look at that," he said. "Each layer of rock is a chapter in the history of the Earth. By taking fossils from different layers, we can tell what happened over the course of millions of years."

"Can you tell why the dinosaurs disappeared?" Ally asked.

"No one's quite sure," Brown replied. "A volcano, an earthquake, a meteor . . . something that made the Earth unlivable for the dinosaurs. There's a layer of ash on these cliffs from sixty-five million years ago. It could be the result of fires that raged across the entire world. That was exactly the same time as when tyrannosaurs, and the rest of the dinosaurs, disappeared."

Ally remembered her idea about mother *T. rexes*. "Do you think they laid eggs?" she asked.

"Tyrannosaurs?" Brown said. "Well, most dinosaurs did. But we've never found any *T. rex* eggs."

"What do you think the eggs would look like?" Ally asked.

But Barnum Brown had already disappeared. Ally was holding tightly to the edge of the bathroom sink.

Whew, Ally thought. All this jumping back and forth in time made her dizzy. Maybe if she left the bathroom she would find her dad. She opened the door—

And looked out once more upon a Cretaceous forest.

"Not again!" Ally exclaimed. She walked out into the thick jungle. Pushing aside a hanging vine, she almost tripped on a hole in the ground.

She looked down and saw that it wasn't a hole. It was an enormous *T. rex* footprint. Ally shivered. I wonder if this means a tyrannosaur is somewhere nearby, she thought.

A loud squawk made her look up. A pteranodon, a large flying reptile, flew out of the trees.

Like a prehistoric airplane, it swooped down at Ally!

Ally ducked.

The pteranodon passed overhead.

"Dad!" Ally called out again.

"Ally!" replied a distant voice.

She pressed on through the thick undergrowth.

A rustling sound made her pause, and she hid behind a stand of palm trees. She peered out.

There in front of her was a nest of dinosaur eggs.

A greedy Ornithomimus was slurping up one of the eggs.

It looked up and saw Ally.

And sprang!

Ally ducked down behind the palms. She expected the Ornithomimus to come after her, but nothing happened. After a moment, she peered out. The Ornithomimus was gone.

This was her big chance. She tiptoed over to the nest and looked down at the eggs.

The eggs looked just like the mysterious rock fossil back in the museum!

These are the biggest eggs I've ever seen, Ally thought. I wonder if this is a *T. rex* nest.

One of the eggs moved. Maybe it was about to hatch!

Without warning, the Ornithomimus rose up behind her. Ally jumped back and fell into the nest. The Ornithomimus lunged at her.

Suddenly the earth shook. And a huge foot slammed into the ground.

lly looked up. An enormous *Tyrannosaurus rex* towered above the nest.
And it looked furious!

But the mother *T. rex* didn't attack Ally. Instead, with a loud roar, it came at the egg-stealer.

The *Ornithomimus* jumped out of the way. But the *T. rex* charged again. The two dinosaurs circled the nest, ready to fight.

Great! Ally thought. And I'm caught right in the middle!

In a flash the Ornithomimus dashed into the nest, grabbed an egg, and darted away.
"Give her back her egg!" Ally shouted.

Growling, the *T. rex* stomped after the smaller dinosaur. Ally followed, scrambling through the underbrush.

The Ornithomimus stopped at the edge of a cliff. With a roar, the mother *T. rex* grabbed the Ornithomimus and flung it into the air. The egg went flying.

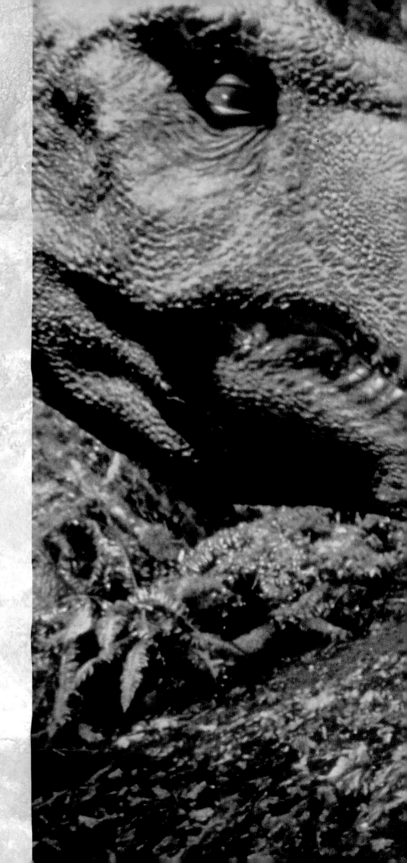

Ally put her hands out and caught the egg.

"I've got it," she yelled.

The tyrannosaur wheeled around and stared at Ally.

Slowly Ally placed the egg at its mother's feet. "Here it is," she said.

The *T. rex* bent down to sniff her egg. Then she gazed back at Ally.

This is my big chance, Ally thought, taking a deep breath.

She reached out—and patted the *T. rex's* nose.

Boom! An asteroid streaked across the sky and crashed into a far-off volcano.

Ally and the mother *Tyrannosaurus rex* jumped and turned. Ally gazed into the distance. A giant wave of gas and dust was moving rapidly through the air. In a moment, it would reach them.

Could this be what caused the extinction of the dinosaurs? Ally wondered.

The *T. rex* looked down at the egg, then out at the approaching cloud. She let out one last mighty roar.

Then a wave of debris smashed into the mother tyrannosaur.

Before Ally's eyes, the *T. rex*'s skin flew off. Its muscles shriveled. Its insides disappeared.

And only the bare bones remained.

Ally looked up at the tyrannosaur's skeleton. She was back in the museum exhibit.

"Ally!" Donald Hayden ran into the hall. "Where have you been? I've been looking all over for you."

"I'm okay, Dad," Ally replied. "I'm back . . . I mean, I'm here."

She knew that if she told her dad what had happened, he'd never believe her. But now that she'd actually met a tyrannosaur, she was eager to do more work on her science project.

Her dad put his arm around Ally as they walked back into the Preparator's lab. "I read part of your project on the mothering behavior of the *T. rex*," he said. "It's really good."

Ally gestured toward the mysterious fossil on the desk. "You know, Dad, I think you're going to find out that's a *T. rex* egg."

"You think so?" Dr. Hayden said. He gathered up his books. "You might be right. Maybe next summer when I go on my dig, you'd like to come along."

"Wow! You really mean it?" Ally said. She grabbed her backpack and turned off the lights. "I can hardly wait!"

The Preparator's lab was silent. The museum cat snoozed on a bookshelf. The fossil egg lay on the desk where Dr. Hayden had left it.

Then the fossil shook. And shook again.

Something was moving inside it, fighting to get out.

The cat opened its eyes and stared. The fossil quaked once again, more violently this time. The cat meowed and ran quickly from the room.

A crack appeared in the rock. It grew wider—and wider.

Something began to crawl out. First a leg. Then a scaly body. Then a head with sharp little teeth.

It was a baby *T. rex* !

Glossary of Terms

ASTEROID: A piece of rock flying through space, left over from the formation of the planets. Occasionally, asteroids come within the Earth's pull of gravity. Then they fall down to the planet. Most burn up in the air before they reach the ground. Some large ones make it all the way to the ground and hit with thunderous explosions. Some scientists think that the impact of a mile-wide asteroid 65 million years ago helped kill off the dinosaurs.

CRETACEOUS: (kri-TAY-shus) The last of the three periods in which the dinosaurs lived is called the Cretaceous Period. It began about 135 million years ago and ended 65 million years ago. *Tyrannosaurus rex* lived during this period.

CYCAD: (SIE-cad) An ancient tree that grew in Cretaceous times. It looked like a palm tree and had fernlike leaves. Some plant-eating dinosaurs ate mainly cycads.

DINOSAURS: The group of animals related to both reptiles and birds. The name means "terrible lizards." When they were first discovered, dinosaurs were thought to be giant, ancient reptiles. They laid eggs, and had scaly hides like reptiles. But most scientists think they were different enough from reptiles to be a separate group of animals by themselves.

DIG SITE: Any place where fossils have been discovered and dug for. Scientists may visit and revisit the same site to dig for more fossils over a period of years.

DRYPTOSAURS: (DRIP-toe-sawrs) Two-legged, meat-eating dinosaurs from the early Cretaceous Period. They grew to about 11 feet long. Dryptosaurs had long, curved, sharp teeth and claws. The name means "tearing lizard," referring to their sharp claws and teeth.

EXTINCTION: A natural process by which animal species die off and disappear. All groups of animals go through extinction. When "dinosaur extinction" is mentioned, it means the time when all of the different dinosaur families had died off. This happened about 65 million years ago.

FIELD STUDY: When scientists go looking for a place to dig up fossils, they study the land to see if older layers of the Earth are exposed. In these older layers they may discover dinosaur bones and other fossils.

FOSSIL: A piece of a once-living thing, either an animal or plant, preserved as stone. Over time, minerals dissolved in water slowly replace the once-living tissue of a plant or animal. After millions of years, the bone or plant has become stone, keeping the same size and shape.

HADROSAURS: (HAD-row-sawrs) Hadrosaurs were a dinosaur family often called the "duckbills." Horny beaks somewhat like a duck's covered their long, flat snouts. Hadrosaurs were plant-eating dinosaurs that ran on two hind legs.

ORNITHOMIMUS: (or-ni-tho-MIME-us) This was a speedy little two-legged dinosaur. Its name means "bird imitator." Ornithomimus was built like a modern ostrich. But it had long front arms instead of wings. It was a swift runner and could probably move as fast as an ostrich—about 40 miles an hour—when it had to. This meat-eater grew to a length of about 12 feet.

PALEONTOLOGIST: (pay-lee-un-TAHL-uh-jist) A scientist who studies fossils to learn about ancient living things.

PREHISTORIC: Referring to the time before humans started to record events. Written records and pictures about people and events are the tools of history. The time before there were records of people and events is called "prehistory."

PTERANODON: (ter-AN-uh-don) A giant flying reptile from the Cretaceous Period. It had a body the size of a turkey, and a wingspan of 27 feet! It had a long toothless beak, and a long bony crest on the back of its head. It had short legs and no tail.

SKELETON: The complete set of bones of an animal.

TROPICS: Area of the Earth near the equator, between the Tropic of Cancer and Tropic of Capricorn. Tropical areas are the hottest on Earth.

TYRANNOSAURUS REX: (tie-ran-uh-SAW-rus REX) A giant two-legged meat-eater. The name means "king tyrant lizard." It grew to 40 to 50 feet long and weighed as much as 6 tons. Tyrannosaurus rex had long, jagged knifelike teeth made for biting through flesh and bones.

UNDERBRUSH: Shrubs, bushes, and small trees growing beneath large trees in a forest.

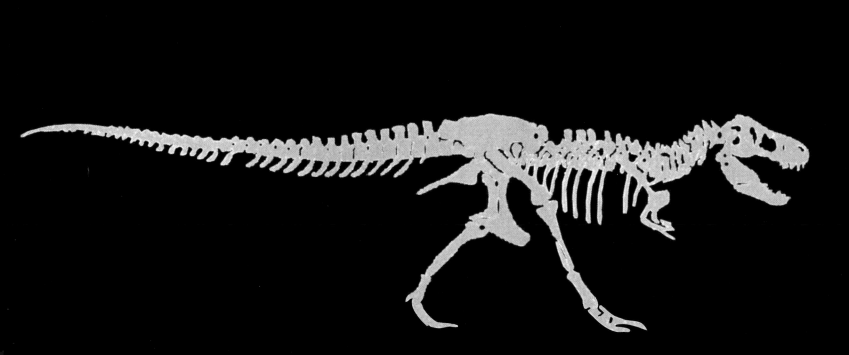